מסורה

ArtScroll Youth Series®

Rabbi Nosson Scherman / Rabbi Meir Zlotowitz

General Editors

עִיר וְקַדִּישׁ מִן שְׁמַיָא נְחִת

לא תשכח מפי ז

Take Me to the

Published by

Mesorah Publications, ltd

קבר רחל

Holy Land

A youngster's tour of Eretz Yisrael

by **Tsivia Yanofsky**

RTSCROLL YOUTH SERIES®

"TAKE ME TO THE HOLY LAND"

© *Copyright 2000 by* Mesorah Publications, Ltd.
First edition – First impression: December, 2000

Published and Distributed by **MESORAH PUBLICATIONS, LTD.**
4401 Second Avenue / Brooklyn, NY 11232 / (718) 921-9000 / Fax: (718) 680-1875 / www.artscroll.com

Distributed in Israel by SIFRIATI / A. GITLER
8 Hayarkon Street / Bnei Brak 51127 / Israel

Distributed in Europe by LEHMANNS
Unit E, Viking Industrial Park / Rolling Mill Road / Jarrow, Tyne & Wear NE32 3DP, England

Distributed in Australia and New Zealand by GOLDS WORLD OF JUDAICA
3-13 William Street / Balaclava Melbourne 3183 / Victoria, Australia

Distributed in South Africa by KOLLEL BOOKSHOP
Shop 8A Norwood Hypermarket / Norwood 2196 / Johannesburg, South Africa

Printed in the United States of America by
Maven Quality Printers / Weehawken NJ
Custom bound by Sefercraft, Inc. / 4401 Second Avenue / Brooklyn N.Y. 11232

ISBN: 1-57819-495-4

Acknowledgements

First and foremost I offer thanks to Hashem for providing me with the opportunity to give Jewish children a taste of the beauty of His land.

I am dedicating this book to my parents, David and Tsila Silberstein who have filled my life with sunshine and laughter from earliest childhood. Their love, encouragement, and true wisdom are forever my inspiration.

I would also like to thank my in-laws, Rabbi Moshe and Sharon Yanofsky, for the distinct pleasure and privilege of being part of a family who are עוסקים בצרכי צבור באמונה of the highest order. They are as special as their reputation – and even more so.

I am grateful as well to my grandmothers, Mrs. Nechama Roth, a second generation Yerushalmi whom we all love very much, may she have a רפואה שלימה and Mrs. Bessi Sinensky, my dear grandmother, whose vitality and wit will keep her forever young.

As I mentioned in the introduction, my children, Avraham Chaim, Rachel, Aharon Shaul, Yecheskel, and Sarah, were instrumental in causing me to write this book with their enthusiasm and interest in the subject matter. My father, as always, was a fount of information, as well as my primary editor.

A special thank you to Rabbi Nochum Braude of Eretz Yisrael and my brother, Chesky Silberstein, for their valuable input.

My husband, Shimon, is of course, my partner and guide in all of life's challenges. (This book was no exception.) May we merit to see much nachas from our children.

Although many people contributed photos, the bulk of these photos came from three special people, Rabbi Jeruchom L. Shapiro, administrator of Beth Jacob of Boro Park, Rabbi Eli Teitelbaum, director of Camp S'dei Chemed, and C.J. Schnitzler. They really enhanced the book and their contribution is greatly appreciated.

An unusual project of this scope required the skill of not just any ordinary publishing company. The challenging photo layout, graphic design and child appeal were no simple matters to achieve. This could only be done by a devoted and exceptionally talented staff such as ArtScroll/Mesorah Publications whose hallmark of excellence is renowned.

Rabbi Meir Zlotowitz and Rabbi Nosson Scherman took a personal interest in this project, and their involvement is quite evident. It was truly a pleasure and privilege to benefit from their sage advice.

My great appreciation to Eli Kroen, Hershy Feuerwerker, Danny Kay and Hindy Goldner. They spent countless hours in designing this work and the final product bears testimony to their consummate skill and genius. I would also like to thank the typing department at Mesorah, Mrs. Tova Finkelman, whose professional proofreading enhanced the manuscript, and Mrs. Rivkah Hamaoui, who helped coordinate the overflow. Most of all this book was made possible by Rabbi Avrohom Biderman, a master coordinator whose infinite patience, wisdom and leadership are worthy of ArtScroll's standard of excellence.

MEDITERRANEAN SEA

ASHER

Rosh Hanikrah

Miron

Acco

Tzefas

MENASHEH

NAFTALI

Teveriah

KINNERET

Haifa

ZEVULUN

YISSACHAR

Chaderah

MENASHEH

Netanyah

Sh'chem

Bnei Brak

Jordan River

Tel Aviv
Yaffo

Petach Tikvah

EFRAIM

GAD

Rechovos

DAN

BINYAMIN

Yericho

Yerushalayim

Ashkelon

Beis Lechem

DEAD SEA

REUVEN

Chevron

YEHUDAH

Gaza

Ein Gedi

Beer Sheva

Masadah

SHIMON

ERETZ YISRAEL AND THE TRANSJORDAN
as divided among the Tribes at the time of Tanach,
showing the locations of today's major cities
and sites featured in this book

Eilat

©2000 Mesorah Publications, Ltd. Reproduction prohibited

Table of Contents

A Letter to Parents   **8**

Introduction   **9**

הַכֹּתֶל הַמַּעֲרָבִי / The Western Wall   **14**

יְרוּשָׁלַיִם / Jerusalem   **26**

שַׁעֲרֵי יְרוּשָׁלַיִם / Jerusalem's Gates   **38**

קֶבֶר רָחֵל / Rachel's Tomb   **43**

מְעָרַת הַמַּכְפֵּלָה / The Machpeilah Cave   **48**

מֵירוֹן / Miron   **57**

צְפַת / Safed   **66**

Water in Eretz Yisrael   **75**

Epilogue: Land of Our Past, Land of Our Future   **81**

A Letter to Parents

A book is seldom the product of three or four months of work. It generally evolves over several years of life's experience. In many instances it is a reflection of the author's dreams and aspirations. Sometimes it may reflect his or her childhood experiences, internalized and presented through an adult perspective.

The inspiration for this book really is my young children who are always clamoring for a story about the Holy Land. They beg and plead for a trip to *Eretz Yisrael,* even offering to save up their own money. A laughable suggestion, but one which I can readily identify with, because my parents have instilled in me a love of the land from my earliest childhood memories. My mother was born in *Eretz Yisrael,* my father grew up there, and somehow, although I grew up in Brooklyn, their homeland always lurked comfortably in the background. It popped up in expressions, stories, pictures, and song. It became part and parcel of my personality — a longing to see and breathe the air of *Eretz Yisrael.* Trips to *Eretz Yisrael* only reinforced and strengthened the bond. I was forever smitten. As I grew older and my own family began to grow, I subconsciously wanted them to develop the feelings I harbored.

My goal in writing this book is quite simple. It is to commit some of this love to writing and perhaps ignite the fire in the minds and hearts of other Jewish children.

This book is not meant to be a historical overview or a comprehensive guide. Nevertheless, much research was done to ensure that the content is accurate. It is written to give our children a taste of the Holy Land, and to ignite within them a spark of desire to see their birthright. This book is intended to be read by children whose imagination and emotions will hopefully soar on the wings of an eagle. It can also be read by parents with their children, interspersing the chapters with their own relationship with *Eretz Yisrael.* A parent's personal story is always most riveting to a child. Yes, they would love to hear how the salt burned Imma's eyes in the *Yam HaMelach,* how the camel chewed her hat in *Midbar Yehudah,* and how the cool waters of the Banias felt. They also want to hear how even Abba cried the first time he stood by the *Kosel,* how Imma and Abba went to *Amukah* within a week of each other, and how Imma cried for her children at *Kever Rachel.* Hopefully, parents will indulge them and indulge their own sense of nostalgia. This precious legacy is the eternal birthright of every Jewish child. If this book will inspire this type of discourse, my purpose will have been fulfilled.

Our Sages tell us, כל המתאבל על ירושלים זוכה ורואה בנחמתה, *Whoever mourns for Yerushalayim will merit to see it in its state of comfort.* It is difficult to mourn the unfamiliar, the distant, the unknown. It is my hope that this book will bring *Eretz Yisrael* closer to home for many Jewish children. In the merit of our longing may we witness the rebuilding of Yerushalayim and the restoration of *Eretz HaKodesh* to its former glory.

Introduction

Did you ever stop to wonder why the mention of *Eretz Yisrael* quickens our pulses and brings smiles to our faces?

We are drawn to *Eretz Yisrael* as if by a magnet. The force pulls us from the four corners of the earth. There is no place on earth, no matter how beautiful, picturesque or fascinating, that means as much to us as *Eretz Yisrael*.

This attraction is a precious legacy from Avraham *Avinu*. Hashem said, "*Lech Lecha* ... go to the land I will show you," and Avraham went. "*Lech Lecha.*" Those words still speak to us. Avraham went unquestioningly, without examining a brochure or leafing through a guidebook. Hashem promised Avraham that his children would inherit the land, and with it the love that connects the Jew to his homeland. Jews throughout the

A young girl walks toward the Cardo, site of an ancient Roman marketplace in Yerushalayim

generations have left their homes and security to fulfill the *mitzvah* of being in *Eretz Yisrael*. Ignoring logic they crossed turbulent seas and trekked across plains and deserts just to kiss the holy soil. Today travel methods are easier, but the joy we experience is thousands of years old. Whether a Jew comes by boat or plane, he is a Jew coming home.

We share this special love with Hashem Himself. "I love all shuls and study halls," says Hashem, "but what do I love most of all? Tzion, Yerushalayim." Yerushalayim is the focus of all of our love and longing, which radiates to and embraces all of the Land of Israel. Every river and stream, each stone and bush is precious.

During the 1930s Jews had difficulty reaching the *Kosel* because of Arab opposition. The British government appointed a commission to investigate. The committee interviewed many people, including some of the great rabbis of the land. A member of the commission asked. "Rabbi, what's the fuss over the Wall? All that is

Kikar Shabbos, a bustling intersection near the Geulah and Meah Shearim neighborhoods of Yerushalayim

It's always the right time to visit Eretz Yisrael.
This Yerushalayim building, originally built to house guests from other countries, is now used as a shul and kollel.
The sundial was designed and constructed by master craftsmen, and still accurately shows the time of day.

Even the camels in Eretz Yisrael have character!

there is a bunch of rocks piled on top of one another." The Rabbi replied, "Just as there are hearts that are made of stone, so there are stones that have a heart." Truly all of *Eretz Yisrael* is the heartbeat of our nation.

We long for the day when we can once again perform all the special *mitzvos* connected to *Eretz Yisrael*. Our fingers yearn to cut and reap, till and plow *admas hakodesh*. Our spiritual limbs are stiff with disuse. May Hashem rebuild the *Beis HaMikdash* speedily in our days, so that we can traverse the length and breadth of *Eretz Yisrael* as we go to Yerushalayim three times a year to bring our offerings and feel the holiness of the *Shechinah*. Wherever we live let us recall the words of Rabbi Yehudah HaLevi, לִבִּי בְמִזְרָח וְאָנֹכִי בְּסוֹף מַעֲרָב, *My heart is in the East* (Yerushalayim) *though I am far to the West.* Like him, we yearn to come home.

Some of the places that will be discussed in this book are *kevarim*, resting places of *tzaddikim*. These places are very holy, and many Jews throughout the generations have gone there to pray, in the hope that the merits of these great *tzaddikim* would help that the prayers would be accepted by Hashem. Some people have the custom of immersing in a *mikveh* before visiting the tombs of *tzaddikim*.

There are many different customs practiced when visiting these holy places. Among them are giving charity at the gravesite, lighting

Har HaMenuchos: Grave of Rabbi Moshe Feinstein, with stones piled on top as is the custom

Har HaMenuchos:
Left, Grave of the
Tchebiner Rav.
Right, praying at
the grave of
R' Aharon of Belz.
Note the stones piled on
top of both graves.

candles next to the grave, and placing pebbles on the tomb-stone. While all these customs are important, most important of all is to remember that a great person is buried in this place, and that one's prayer and behavior have to be worthy. May we merit the return of all our leaders and advisors, the *tzaddikim* of all generations past, speedily in our days.

Grave of the
Kopishinitzer
Rebbe in
Teveriah

הַכֹּתֶל הַמַעֲרָבִי
The Western Wall

הַכֹּתֶל הַמַּעֲרָבִי*
The Western Wall

Kosel HaMaaravi in the snow, a rare sight

In every type of weather — sun, rain, snow or clouds — and at every time of day, the *Kosel* has a special beauty. Jews come from all over the world to pray at the *Kosel*. Many people begin to cry as soon as they come near it. This is just like a child who begins to cry when he sees his mother when he is hurt or upset, or after not having seen her for a long time. So many people come to the *Kosel*, that the stones have become darker from all the tears and fingerprints of Hashem's children. While we can pray anywhere in the world, the *Kosel* is a special place for Jews to run and cry to *Avinu ShebaShamayim,* our Father in Heaven.

The marble squares that make up the plaza in front of the *Kosel* are never empty. Twenty-four hours a day, at midnight or dawn, Jews are there: Young and old, male and female, Sephardic and Ashkenazic, Torah leaders and those who never learned Torah. All come to the *Kosel* to pour out their hearts to Hashem.

A mohel clutching his knife, about to perform a bris at the Kosel HaMaaravi

*Pronounced HaKosel, or HaKotel, HaMaaravi

Women's section of the Kosel HaMaaravi

DID YOU KNOW?

The first *Beis HaMikdash* was built by King Shlomo and stood for four hundred and ten years. It was destroyed by Nevuchadnezar, the Babylonian king who also destroyed Yerushalayim. Today, part of Babylonia is called Iraq. After seventy years the kingdom of Persia, now called Iran, defeated Babylonia. King Koresh of Persia allowed the Jews to go up to Yerushalayim and rebuild the *Beis HaMikdash*. Led by Zerubavel ben Shaaltiel, a group of forty-two thousand Jews went up to rebuild. The Shomronim, non-Jews who lived in *Eretz Yisrael,* became very jealous. They fought with the Jews and tried to stop them from building. They even convinced Achashveirosh, the new king of Persia, to stop the Jews from rebuilding. Only eighteen years later did Daryavesh II, son of Queen Esther and King Achashveirosh, allow the Jews to finish rebuilding the Second *Beis HaMikdash.*

Question Corner

What exactly is the *Kosel HaMaaravi* and why do so many Jews want to pray there?

The *Kosel* is actually the western wall that surrounded the *Har HaBayis,* the Temple Mount. Both the first and second *Beis HaMikdash* were built on the *Har HaBayis*. Jews are not halachically permitted to go onto the *Har HaBayis*, and the closest area a Jew can be is at the *Kosel HaMaaravi*. No wonder that Jews throughout the generations dreamed of praying at the *Kosel*. There were even Jews who traveled by boat and on camels across oceans and deserts, placing themselves in great danger, just to be able to come as close as possible to the *Kosel*.

Doesn't Hashem listen to our prayers anytime, anywhere?

Of course! But the *Kosel* is indeed a special place to pray, as our Sages tell us that Hashem promised that the *Shechinah*, Hashem's Holy Presence, would never move away from the *Kosel HaMaaravi*.

View of Har HaBayis area

Interesting Facts

The holiest part of the *Beis HaMikdash* was the *Kodesh HaKodashim* — the Holy of Holies. The only vessel in the *Kodesh HaKodashim* was the *Aron*. Only the *Kohen Gadol* was allowed to enter the *Kodesh HaKodashim*, once a year on Yom Kippur. The *Kodesh HaKodashim* was on top of a huge rock called the *Even Shesiyah*, the Foundation Rock. Our Sages tell us that the *Even Shesiyah* was the first thing Hashem made when He created the world. It kept getting bigger and bigger until Hashem told it to stop. That is how the planet Earth was made.

Hundreds of years ago, the Muslim Arabs built a mosque on the *Har HaBayis*. A mosque is a place where Muslims pray. On top of the mosque the Muslims built a gold dome which looks like a golden cap. According to most opinions, that mosque was built directly on the rock where the *Kodesh HaKodashim* had been. That is why it is called the Dome of the Rock.

The *Kosel* — which is the western wall around the *Har HaBayis* — was closer to the Holy of Holies in the *Beis HaMikdash* than any of the other walls.

There are some righteous people who will not touch the *Kosel* at all, because of its great holiness. Others have the custom to touch it only after they have purified themselves in a *mikveh*.

Kvitlach placed in the cracks of the Kosel HaMaaravi

Many people are careful not to stick a finger into the cracks between the stones, because the land under the *Kosel* may be part of the *Har HaBayis,* where we are not allowed to be.

If one looks closely at the *Kosel,* one can see thousands of folded pieces of paper with writing in every language. Many different things are written on these papers. People write the names of sick people or their own names together with their problems or prayers for help. These papers are known as *kvitlach* (notes). Many people who come to pray at the *Kosel* and pour out their hearts, stick these small papers into the cracks and pray that Hashem will answer their prayers and requests. The *Chida* writes that when he travelled to Yerushalayim the holy *Ohr HaChaim* gave him a note to put into the *Kosel* on his behalf.

The narrow plaza at the Kosel before the buildings were torn down

IN OUR TIMES

From the 1200's to the 1500's houses were built leaning against the *Kosel.* These buildings even left marks on the *Kosel.* In the 1500's some of the buildings were torn down, while others remained. Only after the war of 1967 was the entire space before the *Kosel* cleared.

It was Teves and rain had not fallen in Yerushalayim in months. The wells were empty. Epidemics broke out. Many took sick and died. The Rav of Yerushalayim, R' Shmuel Salant, and his court decided to proclaim *Erev Rosh Chodesh* Shevat as a day of fasting and prayer. *Minchah* would be prayed at the *Kosel*. All of Yerushalayim was expected to fill the streets and alleys leading to the *Kosel*. A special group was invited, and were promised front row seats closest to the *Kosel*. These were the *tinokos shel bais rabban*, the young school children whose pure prayers would surely rise to the heavenly throne. In those days only a very small area at the *Kosel* was open; the rest of the *Kosel* was covered with Arab houses, so there was very little room for people to pray there.

On Erev Rosh Chodesh, all the roads and alleys leading up to the *Kosel* area were bursting with people. The children, led by their teachers, made their way to the front. The sea of people parted to make way for these honored guests, whose prayers were so very important. The prayers then began. *Tehillim* was recited verse by verse.

Suddenly, a hush fell over the crowd. R' Shneur Zalman, the author of *Sefer Toras Chesed*, was approaching. Due to old age and ill health the rav spent his days at home learning and praying. He slowly made his way with difficulty, wearing his heavy fur hat. As soon as the rav arrived, *Minchah* began. The childish, crying voices of the sweet children kept on chanting וְתֵן טַל וּמָטָר, *Give us rain*. They repeated this at least thirty times.

Minchah was followed by *Maariv*. At the end of the *Maariv* service, the huge throng of children and adults slowly started weaving their way back home. Many followed the Rav of Lublin. When the rav was almost home the skies grew dark and thunder split the air. A minute later heavy torrents of rain started falling. Hashem had answered the prayers of the Jews of Yerushalayim at the *Kosel HaMaaravi*.

Chol HaMoed Succos prayer at the Kosel HaMaaravi

*Cheder children coming
to pray at the Kosel
HaMaaravi — Hashem
especially loves the
prayers of children*

HALACHAH CORNER

There are many things that a Jew does to remember the *Churban* — the destruction of the *Beis HaMikdash*. Even though we never saw the *Beis HaMikdash,* and even though it was destroyed over nineteen hundred years ago, we are still sad that it was destroyed. We cannot even begin to imagine the beauty and glory of the *Beis HaMikdash* and the holiness it brought to the world. When the *Beis HaMikdash* will be rebuilt there will be no more wars and sickness and everyone will follow in the ways of Hashem.

Every day we pray to Hashem to bring *Mashiach* and rebuild the *Beis HaMikdash.* Among the special things one does to remember the *Churban* is to leave a small square on a wall inside the house without paint or plaster. Many homes have the unfinished square right across the doorway, where everyone can easily see it and remember. This is to show that even though we are very happy to have built a house, there is still a part of us that is sad over the *Churban*. A *chassan* (bridegroom) breaks a glass at the *chupah* — in order to remember the *Churban* and show that his happiness is not complete. All of this is in order to fulfill the verse in *Tehillim* — אִם אֶשְׁכָּחֵךְ יְרוּשָׁלָיִם תִּשְׁכַּח יְמִינִי, *If I forget you, O Yerushalayim, let my right hand forget how to move and do things.*

If more than a month has passed since the last time one has seen the *Har HaBayis,* one should tear his clothing when he sees it again. This is called *keriah*, a *tear* on the clothing, over the heart. Tearing one's clothing is a symbol of great sadness, the way people tear their clothing when their closest relatives die. By tearing our clothing we are showing that even though the *Beis HaMikdash* was destroyed so many years ago, we are still very sad today. (At certain times one does not have to tear *keriah* — such as Shabbos and *Yom Tov*, Friday afternoons, Purim, *Chol HaMoed,* etc.)

Two Israeli soldiers praying at the Kosel HaMaaravi

The height of the Kosel HaMaaravi as seen from the ground.

IN OUR TIMES

From 1948 to 1967 the *Kosel* was in the hands of Jordan, an Arab country on the east side of the Jordan River. The Jordanians did not let Jews come into the Arab part of Yerushalayim, and for all those years, Jews could not pray at the *Kosel*. In 1967 there was a Six-Day War between Israel and the Arab countries. The Arabs were ready to attack Israel. They even said they would make all the Jews leave *Eretz Yisrael,* but Hashem helped the Jews and Israel won the war. During the war, on כ״ח אייר, תשכ״ז, the Israeli army recaptured the *Kosel*. Newspapers all over the world showed the famous picture of soldiers looking up at the *Kosel* with love and longing in their eyes. The first army unit that got there radioed back, *"HaKotel Shelanu,* the *Kosel* is ours!" Jews everywhere cried with joy. As soon as the fighting stopped, thousands and thousands of Jews walked through the streets of the old city of Yerushalayim to kiss and pray at the *Kosel*. They were like lost children coming home. After the Six-Day War Jews streamed to the *Kosel* from all over *Eretz Yisrael,* and from all over the world.

The *Kosel* is a place where many people feel a closeness to Hashem. Many people have decided to learn more about

A child walking through the underground tunnels of the Kosel HaMaaravi

Birkas Kohanim at the Kosel HaMaaravi

A miniature model of the Beis HaMikdash and Yerushalayim at the Holyland Hotel in Yerushalayim

Torah and *mitzvos* because of the special feeling they had when visiting the *Kosel*.

Since 1967, much digging has been done at the *Kosel*. The *Kosel* that we see from the floor and up is fifty-one feet high. This is approximately the height of a four-story building. The *Kosel* is also fifty-one feet below the ground; it is exactly double the height that we can actually see. On the left side of the *Kosel*, in the men's section, there is a closed area with two deep enclosed pits. By looking down into these pits one can see the other half of the *Kosel*, which is hidden under the ground.

The largest stone of the *Kosel* wall discovered by the diggers is about forty-two feet long and ten feet high. It weighs over five hundred tons — a million pounds! This is about the weight of more than 300 cars. We have no idea how the Jews in those days were able to lift such weighty stones without heavy machinery.

Were you ever in Yerushalayim for *Chol HaMoed*? If so you would have been able to join thousands of Jews from all over *Eretz Yisrael* and even all over the world. These Jews want to be at the *Kosel* for *Birkas Kohanim*. The *Kohanim* stand before the *Kosel* wrapped in their *talleisim* and bless the thousands of Jews standing before them with the same blessing that Hashem gave to Aharon and his children … יְבָרֶכְךָ ה׳ וְיִשְׁמְרֶךָ. The sight of hundreds of *Kohanim* blessing tens of thousands of people at the *Kosel* is very moving. One can only imagine what it must have been like to see our nation standing in the courtyard of the *Beis HaMikdash* and praying.

Our Sages explain that in every generation we are helping to rebuild the *Beis HaMikdash*. Every time we share with our friends, stand up for an older person, pray with concentration, or help our mother or father with a smile (especially when we're not in the mood), we are adding spiritual bricks to the third *Beis HaMikdash*. We are fortunate today to have the *Kosel HaMaaravi*, but we long for the fulfillment of וְתֶחֱזֶינָה עֵינֵינוּ בְּשׁוּבְךָ לְצִיּוֹן … **May our eyes gaze upon Your return, Hashem, to Yerushalayim.**

Praying at the Kosel HaMaaravi

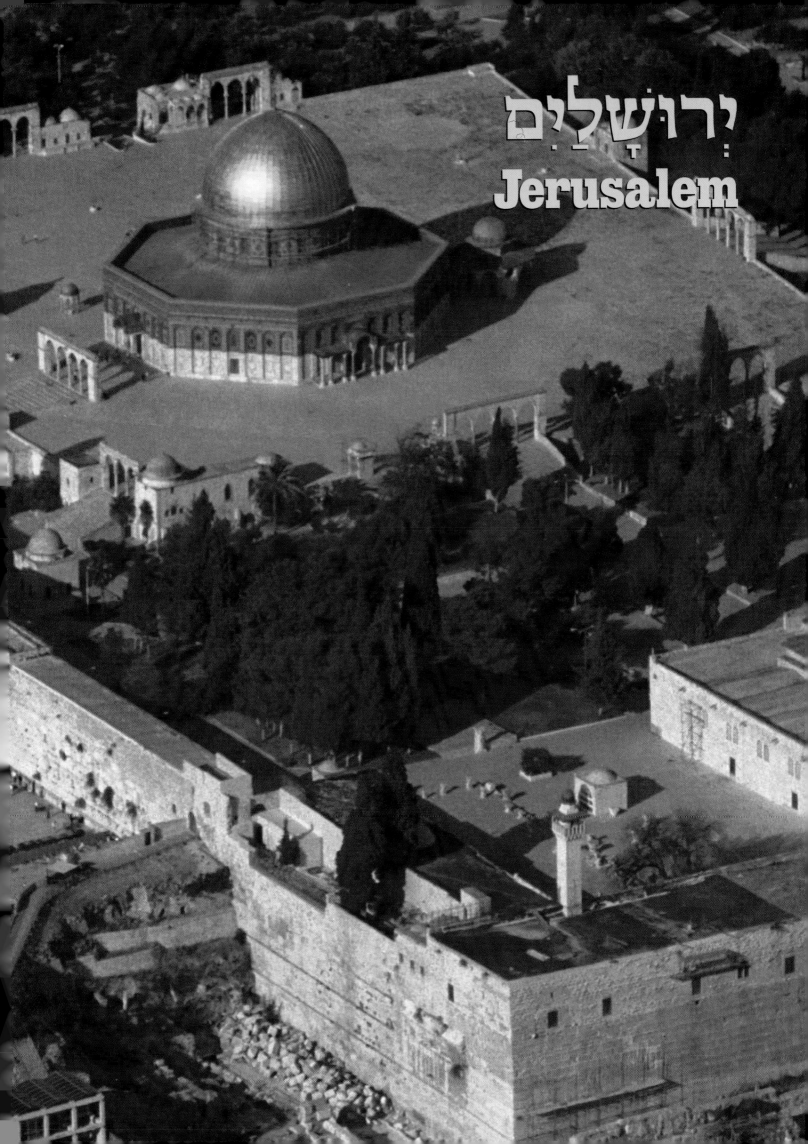

יְרוּשָׁלַיִם
Jerusalem

A boy wearing Yerushalmi Yom Tov garb walking through the streets of Me'ah Shearim on Chol HaMoed Succos.

יְרוּשָׁלַיִם *
Jerusalem

The Churvah of Rabbi Yehudah HaChassid

There are many old and beautiful shuls in the holy city of Yerushalayim. Great people such as the *Ramban, Ohr HaChaim* and the *Rashash* prayed in these shuls. It is a very special feeling to stand and pray in such places. As we pray, we hope that the merit of these holy people help our prayers reach the heavenly throne.

One of the most famous shuls in Yerushalayim has a very strange name. It is known as the *Churvah*, which means ruin in *Lashon HaKodesh*. The shul was originally named after Rabbi Yehudah HaChassid, a great *tzaddik* and a very well-known leader. He was famous for his speeches about how a Jew should act to bring the *Geulah*, the final redemption, closer.

In the 1700's R' Yehudah led a group of over one thousand Jews up to *Eretz Yisrael* from Poland. In those days people traveled by boat, and the trip was often dangerous and difficult. When they arrived in Yerushalayim, they borrowed large amounts of money from the Arabs in order to build a shul. A few months later, while they were in the middle of building, a terrible plague broke out in Yerushalayim. Many Jews became sick and died. R' Yehudah HaChassid was one of them.

The Polish Jews who had followed R' Yehudah lost all interest in building the shul without their leader. Some people from the group even left Yerushalayim and went to live in Tzefas. Those remaining could not pay back the money they owed the Arabs. The Arabs were very angry. One night they burned the shul

Remains of the Churvah Shul

Question Corner

What did the shul look like?

It had a huge dome on top, a beautifully carved *Aron Kodesh* and many very large and elegant windows. There was a very large silver menorah that stood by one of the windows.

---

*Pronounced *Yerushalayim*

*Beis Knesses HaRamban
with the arch of the Churvah
directly behind it*

down to the ground. For about one hundred years the shul was just a burnt pile of stones, so people began calling it the *Churvah*, the Ruin.

In the early 1800's there was a terrible earthquake in Tzefas. Houses were destroyed and many people died. Many Jews left Tzefas and came to live in Yerushalayim. They finally paid off the debt that was owed to the Arabs for the building of R' Yehudah HaChassid's shul, but they still did not have money to rebuild the shul.

At that time, there was a European family by the name of Rothschild, which was both rich and generous. They gave a lot of money both in Europe and *Eretz Yisrael* to help needy Jews. The Rothschilds donated a lot of money to rebuild the shul.

Once rebuilt, the shul was truly magnificent. Even so the shul was still known as the *Churvah*, a place of ruins.

DID YOU KNOW?

- In the courtyard of the shul was the famous Eitz Chaim yeshivah, the yeshivah of many children who would grow up to become the future leaders of *Eretz Yisrael*.

The Russian Czar who lived in St. Petersburg once ordered a suit from a Jewish tailor. The Czar sent a servant who was about his size to try on the suit. The tailor noticed the servant threading a needle into one of the pockets. When the servant left, the tailor examined the pocket and discovered a needle with powder on it. The powder was tested and discovered to be poison! The servant had wanted to poison the czar. When the tailor told the czar what he had found, the czar gave him a large amount of silver as a reward for saving his life. The tailor had a menorah made from the silver. He sent the menorah as a gift to the famous *Churvah* shul in Yerushalayim.

Even in faraway Russia, a Jew wanted to have a portion in *Eretz Yisrael*.

The name *Churvah* seems to have been prophetic. In 1948, during the War of Independence, the Arabs bombed the shul, as well as most of the shuls in the Jewish Quarter of Yerushalayim. They destroyed it completely, together with the famous Eitz Chaim Yeshivah.

The *Churvah* once more became a ruin and remains that way until this very day. Only an arch was built over the remains of the shul, as a reminder of the dome that once was.

Beit HaKnesset Beit-El

The *Beit-El* shul was famous in Yerushalayim for being a center for *Mekubalim*, people who study the secrets of the Torah. These holy men would learn Kabbalah twenty-four hours a day in eight-hour shifts in this shul. Many times when there was a tragedy or sickness in Yerushalayim, the people would run to the shul and beg the *tzaddikim* learning there to pray for them. It is said that many times salvation came about from those prayers.

There was a yeshivah started by R' Gedaliah Chivan, which learned in this shul for two hundred years.

Ornate doorway of
Beit Knesset Beit El
fashioned by master craftsmen

STORY CORNER

S ar Shalom Sharabi was already a Torah scholar and kabbalist when he was still a young man living in Yemen. He was forced to leave Yemen and came to Yerushalayim. He went to the Yeshivat Beit El and asked R' Gedaliah Chivan for a job. He did not tell R' Gedaliah about his own great knowledge of Torah and Kabbalah. R' Gedaliah gave him a job as the *shamash* (caretaker) of the shul. Every day the modest young man would straighten the benches and sweep the room, all the while listening carefully to the *shiurim* and words of Torah. Nobody paid much attention to the silent young man. One day R' Gedaliah looked very upset. He was not able to explain a difficult passage in the *Sefer HaChaim,* a book of Kabbalah. He dismissed the class and everyone went home.

Sar Shalom, who had been listening quietly all along, wrote a few words on a note, and stuck it in the book. The next time R' Gedaliah gave a *shiur* he noticed the note and his eyes lit up with happiness. This happened again and again, but no one could guess the identity of the secret scholar. Channah, the daughter of the Rosh Yeshivah R' Gedaliah, decided to solve the mystery. She watched the yeshivah from her window, until one day she saw Sar Shalom in the act. She quickly ran to tell her father. R' Gedaliah told Sar Shalom that the time had come to reveal his greatness. Sar Shalom married Channah, and after the death of his father-in-law, he became the Rosh Yeshivah of Yeshivat Beit-El.

IN OUR TIMES

In 1948 when the Arabs destroyed much of the Jewish quarter, they burst into *Beit Knesset Beit-El*. Part of the ceiling immediately fell down, killing the Arab soldiers. Today the shul is fully rebuilt and Kabbalah is still studied within the walls of this revered site.

Grave of Rashash,
R' Sholom Sharabi,
on Har HaZeisim

Har HaZeisim. At the lower left is the tomb of the Prophet Zechariah

Har HaZeisim

Har HaZeisim (Mount of Olives) is the mountain directly across from the *Har HaBayis*. From the mountaintop one can get a beautiful view of the *Makom HaMikdash*, the place where the *Beis HaMikdash* stood. *Har HaZeisim* is called by this name because of the many olive trees that grew on the mountain.

During the time of the Second *Beis HaMikdash*, the Sanhedrin used signals to let people know when it was Rosh Chodesh, the new month. The signals were big fires that were lit on a series of mountaintops going all the way to Bavel. The first mountain upon which a fire was lit was *Har HaZeisim*.

Har HaZeisim has the most famous Jewish cemetery in the world. Even today, many Jews long to be buried there. New graves are dug on top of old graves, as many of the very old ones have sunk deep into the mountain. All kinds of Jews are buried here: kings, prophets, leaders and ordinary Jews. Some of the burial places are from the time of King David.

Question Corner

Why do so many people throughout the generations want to be buried on *Har HaZeisim*?

Tradition tells us that when *Mashiach* comes the bodies of all buried Jews will roll through underground tunnels to *Har HaZeisim*. When they arrive under *Har HaZeisim*, a shofar will be blown and all will rise up and live again.

For this reason, for thousands of years Jews have wanted their final resting place to be among the rocks of this mountain.

The tomb on Mount Zion, said to be that of King David.

CORNER

Among the many holy graves found on Har HaZeisim is the tomb of the *Ohr HaChaim HaKadosh.*

Who was the *Ohr HaChaim?*

The *Ohr HaChaim HaKadosh* was born in Morocco in 1696. Even at a young age it was clear that the *Ohr HaChaim* was a great scholar and a holy person.

Between 1948 and 1967, the Old City of Yerushalayim was under Arab control. During this time the Arabs decided to build on *Har HaZeisim,* where thousands of Jews are buried. They brought a tractor and began destroying the gravestones, so that the ground would be flat. When the tractor reached the grave of the *Ohr HaChaim* it suddenly overturned. The Arabs thought that the tractor had hit a big rock. They sent another tractor and the same thing happened. After the third tractor overturned, the Arabs realized that someone very holy was buried here. They were too scared to try again, and they left the grave in peace. When you go to *Eretz Yisrael* and come to pray at the grave of the *Ohr HaChaim,* you will notice that no gravestones are standing on one side of the *Ohr HaChaim's* grave.

Jews gathered on Har HaZeisim for a funeral.

There is a very unusual-looking building at the foot of *Har HaZeisim.* This small building catches the eye of all passersby. It is called Yad Avshalom. Yad Avshalom is really a monument. A monument is a small

Points to Ponder:

Our Sages tell us that because David did not rebuke Avshalom as much as he should have, Avshalom became wicked. When our parents try to teach us how to behave properly we should try and realize that this is for our own benefit, even if sometimes our parents are forced to punish us. This is not always so easy. Sometimes we wish that our parents wouldn't always tell us what to do. However, if we remember that our parents love us and seek only our benefit, it will be easier to appreciate the valuable words of advice they give us.

Many people pass by Yad Avshalom and think about a father s power of forgiveness. As R' Chaim Shmuelevitz used to pray, may Hashem truly forgive a rebellious nation!

building or statue built to remember a certain person or important event.

Avshalom was one of King David's sons. Since his three sons died, Avshalom did not have anyone to continue his name. Therefore he built a monument in his name during his own lifetime, and called it Yad Avshalom — which it is called to this day.

Avshalom led a very tragic life. He was a rebellious son who fought with his father, David, King of Israel. He wanted to become the king while his father was still alive. He was even ready to kill his father in order to become king. He managed to gather a huge army together. Avshalom was a *nazir*. (A *nazir* is a person who serves Hashem in a special way. He does not cut his hair, come near a dead body or drink wine. He is even careful not to go through a vineyard!) During the battle against his father's troops, Avshalom rode on a donkey. While he was riding,

The tomb of Avshalom on Har HaZeisim

his long hair became entangled in a tree. This trapped him and allowed David's soldiers to kill him. Even though Avshalom caused his father David so much grief and embarrassment, David was still very sad when he was told of his son's death. He called out "אַבְשָׁלוֹם בְּנִי בְנִי". He mentioned the word "בְּנִי" — my son — eight times. The *Gemara* explains that every time he said this David raised Avshalom from each of the seven levels of *Gehinnom*, and with the eighth "בְּנִי" he brought him up to *Gan Eden*.

Whenever R' Chaim Shmuelevitz *zt"l* used to pray at Yad Avshalom he would say "*Ribono shel Olam,* when a person says 'I forgive you' to his friend very often he doesn't really mean it. Only a father can truly forgive his son. Look at Avshalom. Even though he caused his father so much pain and sadness, David truly forgave him. *Ribono shel Olam* — You are our Father. Please say that You forgive us, Your children, the Jewish nation."

Interesting Facts

Many years ago there was a custom in Yerushalayim to pass by the Yad Avshalom monument and throw a stone. This was done to mock a son who rebelled against his father.

שַׁעֲרֵי יְרוּשָׁלַיִם
Jerusalem's Gates

There are eight famous gates which are part of the wall surrounding the Old City of Yerushalayim. Most sections of the wall are not part of the original wall that stood during the time of the first and second *Batei Mikdash*. The present wall was built during the Turkish rule in the 1500s. It was built around the Old City for protection from enemies. For this reason the gates of the wall were built at a slight angle so that enemies could not shoot or gallop straight into the city.

שַׁעַר יַפוֹ/*
Jaffa Gate

Shaar Yaffo is in the western wall surrounding the Old City. It is probably called Shaar Yaffo as this was the gate through which people would leave to travel from Yerushalayim to Yaffo. Although Yaffo is far from Yerushalayim, it was considered a very important city, as it was the closest port to Yerushalayim.

When merchandise, such as building materials or spices, was sent to *Eretz Yisrael* by sea, the boat would dock at the port city of Yaffo. From there the items would be brought by horse and wagon to Yerushalayim. Shaar Yaffo is right near the Tower of David. It is said that King David may have built this tower, although we have no proof for this. Shaar Yaffo is the closest gate to the business center of the new city of Yerushalayim, which was built outside of the walls of the Old City.

*Pronounced *Shaar Yaffo*

שַׁעַר צִיּוֹן*/Zion Gate

Shaar Tzion is in the southern wall surrounding the Old City of Yerushalayim. It is called by this name because it is right near Mount Tzion, where, according to tradition, King David may have been buried. If one looks closely above the gate, two small openings can be seen. These small openings were used to pour boiling water on enemies trying to enter the city. This is the closest gate to the Rova HaYehudi, the Jewish Quarter of the Old City.

שַׁעַר הָאַשְׁפּוֹת**/Dung Gate

Shaar HaAshpos is translated as the Dung Gate. This is indeed a strange name for a gate. The Tosefta comments that there is no gate more lowly or degraded than this one, since it was through this gate that the garbage would be taken outside the city. However, this is the only gate which has the distinct honor of having its name mentioned in *Tanach*, in the book of Nechemiah.

During the Six-Day War the Israeli soldiers entered through this gate on their way to free the Jewish Quarter.

It is also the closest gate to the plaza of the *Kosel HaMaaravi*. Today most people come to the *Kosel* via this gate.

*Pronounced *Shaar Tzion*
**Pronounced *Shaar HaAshpos* or *HaAshpot*

שַׁעַר הָרַחֲמִים*/Gate of Mercy

Shaar HaRachamim can be translated as the Gate of Mercy. This is because for hundreds of years Jews would pray at this gate, begging Hashem for mercy.

This is the only gate in Jerusalem's wall to have a double arch. *Maseches Sofrim* explains that this is because King Shlomo built it as two separate gates. There was a beautiful custom in Yerushalayim for bridegrooms to sit by one of the gates. Fellow Jews would go there to celebrate with these joyful young men. Mourners and outcasts would sit at the other gate, where the people would come and comfort them.

This gate overlooks the Valley of Yehoshafat, where in the future Hashem will judge all of the nations of the world.

The book *Kaftor VaFerach* states that when the Divine presence of Hashem left the *Har HaBayis,* it left through these gates. These gates are now sealed. The author of the book says he was in Yerushalayim in the 1200s when the Arabs tried to break through the gate. A terrible earthquake shook Yerushalayim violently, and only stopped after the Arabs left the gate alone.

---

*Pronounced *Shaar HaRachamim*

שַׁעַר הָאֲרָיוֹת*/Lions' Gate

Shaar HaArayos, or the Lions' Gate, is in the eastern wall surrounding the Old City. It is called by this name as there are two pair of lions carved on each side. Legend has it that the two pairs of lions were carved by Suleiman the Magnificent, the Turkish ruler. Suleiman's father appeared to him in a dream to rebuke him for not fortifying and repairing the wall around the Old City. He threatened that unless the city was properly protected, Suleiman would be held responsible, and wild lions would attack him. To remember his dream, Suleiman carved pairs of lions on each side of the gate.

שַׁעַר שְׁכֶם**/ Damascus Gate

Shaar Sh'chem, or the Damascus Gate, is in the northern wall surrounding the Old City. This was the first gate a traveler from Sh'chem would encounter. This gate is the most magnificent of all the gates and has an interesting decoration along the entire top of the gate.

*Pronounced *Shaar HaArayos or HaArayot*   **Pronounced *Shaar Sh'chem*

שַׁעַר הַפְּרָחִים*/
Gate of Flowers

Shaar Haperachim, or the Gate of Flowers, is in the northern section of the wall surrounding the Old City. It is also known as Herod's Gate. Many believe that Herod built the gate, because the distinctive stones are very similar to the style of stones that Herod had used in his buildings. Herod is most famous for helping refurbish the second *Beis HaMikdash*. It is called the Gate of Flowers because of the flower decorations on its top and side.

שַׁעַר הֶחָדָשׁ**/
The New Gate

The New Gate has this name because it was the most recent gate to be opened in the walls of the Old City. It was built at the end of the 1800s by Turkish Sultan Abdul Hammid in order to allow people who were settling outside the city walls easier access to the Old City. It is not mentioned very often, since it is not located near any major streets or intersections, and is used much less than the other gates are.

*Pronounced *Shaar HaPerachim*
**Pronounced *Shaar HeChadash*

קֶבֶר רָחֵל*
Rachel's Tomb

Rachel was one of the four mothers of the Jewish people. We call her Rachel *Imeinu*, which means "Our Mother, Rachel." When Yaakov *Avinu* met Rachel, he wanted to marry her. Her father, Lavan, said that he would give Yaakov and Rachel permission to marry — but only after Yaakov worked for him for seven years. That is a very long time, but Yaakov knew that Rachel was his predestined wife, so he was happy to do it.

Sign leading to Kever Rachel in three languages, Hebrew, Arabic and English

Lavan was not honest. At the end of seven years of work, when Yaakov was ready to marry Rachel, Lavan tricked him. Instead of bringing Rachel to the wedding, Lavan brought her sister Leah.

What should Rachel do? She and Yaakov had suspected that Lavan might try to fool them, so they had made up secret signals with each other. If Leah did not know the signals, Yaakov would know she was trying to fool him. He would get angry, and Leah would be ashamed.

Rachel didn't want her sister to be embarrassed. She gave Leah the signals. Yaakov did not realize that his bride was Leah until the next day. After the week of *Sheva Berachos*, Yaakov agreed to work for Lavan for another seven years; and Lavan then let him marry Rachel, as well. Rachel and Leah were twins who were twenty-two at the time of their marriage to Yaakov.

Over the years, Leah gave birth to six sons and a daughter, but Rachel did not have children. Finally, after much pain and prayer, she had a son whom she named Yosef. Six years later, she had another son, Binyamin — and then she died, when she was only thirty-six years old.

---

*Pronounced *Kever Rachel*

Points to Ponder:

Rachel *Imeinu* taught us how important it is to keep someone else from being ashamed. We must learn that lesson well.

Yaakov did not bury Rachel in *Me'aras HaMachpelah*, the burial place of the other *Avos* and *Imahos*. Instead he buried her along the way to Beis Lechem, a city near Yerushalayim. Many years later, when Yaakov was in Egypt right before his death, he called Yosef to his bedside. He made Yosef promise that he would take Yaakov's bones out of Egypt and bury him in *Me'aras HaMachpeilah*. Yaakov told Yosef, "I know you feel badly that I buried your mother Rachel along the way. But I want you to know that I did this by Hashem's command, so that she should be able to help her children when they are taken away from their land." Yosef himself, when he was taken to Egypt as a slave, stopped off at his mother's graveside to beg for mercy. He was led on a camel, and when he reached his mother's grave he fell on it, crying. Yosef then heard a voice speaking to him: "Do not fear, because Hashem is with you. Go down to Egypt."

After the first *Beis HaMikdash* was destroyed, the Jews were taken in chains to Bavel by the soldiers of General Nevuzaradan. They stopped at Rachel's grave and cried out like children to their mother. Rachel's soul came out and קוֹל בְּרָמָה נִשְׁמַע — a voice was heard in heaven. It was Rachel crying for her children. She called out, "Master of the World: You know that Yaakov and I were supposed to be married, but I gave my secret signals to Leah so that she should not be shamed. I was not jealous of my sister and was kind to her, even though I thought I was losing my chance to marry Yaakov. Hashem — are You jealous of the idols that the Jewish people bow to? If I was not jealous — why should You be?"

The velvet cover on Kever Rachel, soaked with so many Jewish tears.

When Hashem heard this special prayer, He responded and said to her, מִנְעִי קוֹלֵךְ מִבֶּכִי וְעֵינַיִךְ מִדִּמְעָה. Stop your voice from crying out and your eyes from shedding tears. I promise you that I will reward you for your actions and I will bring the Jewish people back to their land." That was why Yaakov buried Rachel on the roadside. Ever since then, until today, many many Jews come to *Kever Rachel* to pray and beg Hashem for help.

What does Kever Rachel look like?

Yaakov and his sons (the *shevatim*) built a monument on top of Rachel's grave. Each one of the *Shevatim* put down a stone, and Yaakov placed a stone on top of all of them.

Later on ...

In the 1100's, Christian Crusaders came upon *Kever Rachel*. It still had those eleven stones on it. They put up four columns around the grave and put a white dome on top of them.

Kever Rachel before the large stone building was built around it for security purposes.

A WORD FROM THE WISE:

R' Chaim Shmuelevitz asked. "Why did Hashem respond to the Jews only because of Rachel? Was not Avraham willing to sacrifice his son? Was Yitzchak not ready to sacrifice himself? Why only Rachel?" Reb Chaim explained, "People usually do not mind giving up everything for Hashem, sometimes even their lives, but they get very angry if they lose out to another person. Even though Rachel was giving Yaakov to Leah, she did it anyway — just so her sister should not be ashamed! Because she did that, she was able to make Hashem respond to the Jewish people and promise to help them."

More recently ...

About one hundred fifty years ago, there was a British Jew named Sir Moses Montefiore. He was very rich and did many things to help the Jewish people. Once, he and his wife went to *Eretz Yisrael*. In those days, *Eretz Yisrael* was ruled by Turkey. The Montefiores got permission from the Turkish government to fix *Kever Rachel*. They cleaned it and built a beautiful stone building over the site. It had a big room where travelers could rest and eat something, if they were tired and hungry. From then on, the Turks allowed Jews to have control of the site.

The chariot of Sir Moses Montefiore, used on his travels through Eretz Yisrael in the 1800s

In Our Times

In 1996, the government of Israel built a large stone building around the site, so that visitors would be safe. Even though the outside of *Kever Rachel* now looks different, it is still the same holy place that Jews have been visiting for hundreds of years.

Kever Rachel as it appears today, with a large new building erected for security purposes

Kever Rachel is most often visited on the 11th of Cheshvan, the *yahrtzeit* of Rachel *Imeinu*, and also on other special days of prayer, such as *Aseres Yemei Teshuvah, Erev Rosh Chodesh* and fast days. Men, women and children come and touch the velvet cover on the grave, which has the verse קוֹל בְּרָמָה נִשְׁמַע in gold lettering.

Women who have no children cry out to Rachel *Imeinu*. She knows exactly how they feel, because she too had no children for so many years. Orphans without parents come and pour out their hearts to Rachel, whose two sons were left without a mother at such a young age; Yosef was six and Binyamin was a newborn baby. We can imagine how her soul prayed to Hashem for her little boys. Now surely she prays for the children who come to *Kever Rachel* to pray and pour out their hearts to Hashem.

So many different kinds of Jews, many who look different from one another, come to cry out to Rachel and beg her to go before Hashem. Surely Hashem places all of the precious tears of His beloved Jewish people in a special cup. When that cup will be filled to the top, וְשָׁבוּ בָנִים לִגְבוּלָם — Rachel's children will return to their land forever.

Kever Rachel as it was found just after the Six-Day War.

Interesting Facts

• Some have a custom to wind a red thread around *Kever Rachel* while saying *Tehillim*. The string is then worn around the wrist. This is supposed to protect the person from harm.

• When Rabbi Chaim Shmuelevitz *zt"l* would enter *Kever Rachel* to pray, he used to say quietly, "מאַמע, חַיים'קע איז דאָ, Mother, Chaim'ke is here." He was one of the greatest *roshei yeshivah* in the world, but when he came to *Kever Rachel*, he felt like a little boy crying to his mother.

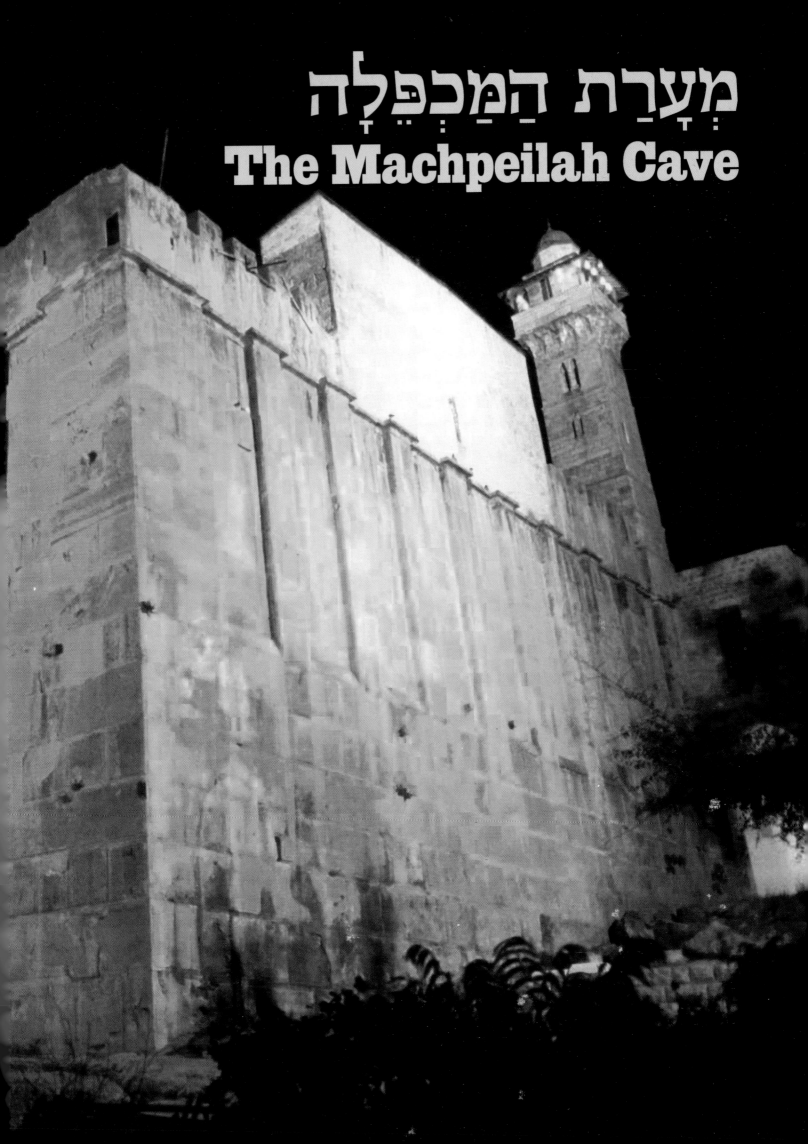

מְעָרַת הַמַכְפֵּלָה
The Machpeilah Cave

Praying at the grave of Yitzchak

מְעָרַת הַמַּכְפֵּלָה*
The Machpeilah Cave

The *Me'aras HaMachpeilah,* in Chevron, is one of the holiest burial places in the entire world. Avraham and Sarah, Yitzchak and Rivkah, and Yaakov and Leah are buried there. The father and mother of all mankind, Adam and Chavah, are buried there as well.

The *Midrash* relates that three times a day, a gentle wind enters the *Me'aras HaMachpeilah* and blows over the tombs of our *Avos* and *Imahos.* They are then awakened and pray for their children, the Jewish people.

For thousands of years, Jews have come to pray at this holy site.

---

*Pronounced *Me'aras,* or *Me'arat,* HaMachpeilah

The Me'aras HaMachpeilah in Chevron

Question Corner

How was the *Me'aras HaMachpeilah* found?

The Zohar tells us that when the three angels came to visit Avraham after his *bris* he wanted to prepare a meal for them. The calf he wanted to serve ran away into a cave and Avraham followed it. As he entered, he smelled the most pleasant fragrance in the world! Avraham saw Adam and Chavah buried in the cave. Adam had originally chosen this place to bury Chavah because it had the special fragrance of *Gan Eden,* the place where Adam and Chavah lived before they sinned by eating from the tree of knowledge. After they sinned they were sent out. But they had never forgotten the beautiful aroma of *Gan Eden.*

Brass gate in the hall of Avraham and Sarah. It is believed that the graves of Avraham and Sarah are located beyond these gates.

The holy *Alshich*, who learned many secrets of the Torah, lived over four hundred years ago. He said that the *Me'aras HaMachpeilah* is the entrance to *Gan Eden*.

When Avraham smelled the delicious fragrance and saw Adam and Chavah buried there, he immediately wanted the cave as a burial place for his family.

Many years later when his wife Sarah died, Avraham went to Ephron HaChiti, who owned the field and cave. Avraham bought the field and the cave for four hundred giant silver coins — a very large sum of money in those days!

The last couple to be buried in the *Me'aras HaMachpeilah* was Yaakov and Leah. Rachel was not buried with Yaakov in the *Me'aras HaMachpeilah*; she was buried on the way to Beis Lechem.

Before Yaakov died, he asked Yosef to promise that he would not bury him in Egypt. Yaakov wanted to be buried in the *Me'aras HaMachpeilah.*

After Yaakov died, his sons surrounded his coffin with crowns. When Yishmael and Eisav heard that Yaakov would be buried in the *Me'aras HaMachpeilah,* they came to fight for the burial place. However, when they saw the crown of Yosef they did not fight. They were afraid of him. Instead, they removed their own crowns and placed them on the coffin of Yaakov, with the other crowns. Altogether, thirty-six crowns were on the coffin. But Eisav still wanted the *Me'aras HaMachpeilah* for himself. He ran there, and when the brothers reached the cave, Eisav stood blocking the entrance. The brothers did not want to fight with him. They reminded him that he had lost his right to the *Me'arah* when he sold his birthright to Yaakov. Eisav demanded to see the written contract, but it was in Egypt. Naftali, who was swift as a deer, ran to Egypt to bring the contract.

Chushim, the son of Dan, saw this whole scene. Chushim was deaf and could not understand what was going on. He asked his cousins the reason for the delay. When they told him he became angry. "Should grandfather lie here in disgrace until Naftali returns?" he asked. Immediately he cut off Eisav's head. The *Midrash* relates that the head rolled into the *Me'arah*. Eisav had the honor of having his head buried in this holy place as a reward for the special way he had honored his father.

Interesting Facts

• Chevron is also known as Kiryat Arba, *the City of Four,* because of the four couples that are buried there: Adam and Chavah, Avraham and Sarah, Yitzchak and Rivkah, and Yaakov and Leah.

Question Corner

Me'aras HaMachpeilah means the "doubled cave."

Why is it called by this name? Because there are two pairs of *Avos* and *Imahos* buried there. Also because the cave had two stories — a bottom floor with an attic on top.

Points to Ponder:

Can you figure out why so many people have the custom of going to the grave of a *tzaddik* to pray on the day of a yahrtzeit?

שרה — א' אלול
יצחק — ט"ו ניסן
יעקב — ט"ז תשרי

שְׁאַל אָבִיךָ וְיַגֵּדְךָ זְקֵנֶיךָ וְיֹאמְרוּ לָךְ — Ask your parents and grandparents; they will be glad to explain why, and maybe they will even tell you stories about the burial places of relatives who passed away.

Ruins at Elonei Mamre, dwelling place of Avraham and Sarah

Question Corner

Moshe said that the city of Chevron would belong to Calev. Why?

Calev went to the *Me'aras HaMachpeilah* in Chevron, to pray that Hashem save him from the evil plan of the spies. When he returned, Moshe promised him that he would receive Chevron as his portion in *Eretz Yisrael*.

What does *Me'aras HaMachpeilah* look like?

The graves of our *Avos* and *Imahos* are under the ground. Above them is a large and beautiful building. Experts believe that King Hordos constructed the building during the time of the Second *Beis HaMikdash*.

In the building itself are three large halls — the halls of Avraham and Sarah, Yitzchak and Rivkah, and Yaakov and Leah. The largest one is the hall of Yitzchak and Rivkah, where the Muslims pray. Truthfully, though, we cannot be sure which hall is built on top of which grave.

The *Me'aras HaMachpeilah* is not considered holy only by the Jews. Christians and especially Muslims come to pray there, as both consider themselves children of Avraham, through Yishmael and Eisav.

From the 1200's to the 1900's, for seven hundred years, the Muslims controlled the site and would not allow Jews to enter the building. They allowed Jews to go up only to the "seventh step" outside the building to pray, but not any closer.

A few times during the seven hundred years, some Jews were able to bribe Muslim guards to allow them to enter the cave. Those that did go, risked their lives to pray at the cave of the *Avos* and *Imahos*.

DID YOU KNOW?

• **A**ccording to the *Midrash*, the grave of Yishai which is across the square from *Me'aras HaMachpeilah* is directly connected to *Me'aras HaMachpeilah*.

Who was Yishai?

Yishai was the father of King David, and the grandson of Boaz and Rus. Our sages tell us that he is one of only four people who never committed a sin!

Some people who came to pray at the *Me'aras HaMachpeilah* decided to see if it was true that the grave of Yishai was connected to the cave. They threw a chicken into the cave of Yishai and after a few minutes it came out the side of *Me'aras HaMachpeilah*!

• **W**hen the Jewish people were in the desert, they asked Moshe to send spies to *Eretz Yisrael* to see what kind of land it was. Hashem gave Moshe permission to do it, even though He had already told *Bnei Yisrael* that it was a very good land. The *nesi'im,* the leaders of each tribe, were sent. Ten of the twelve spies decided to say bad things about *Eretz Yisrael*. Only Calev ben Yephuneh and Yehoshua bin Nun had faith in Hashem. When Calev wanted Hashem to help him resist the other spies, he went to pray at the *Me'aras HaMachpeilah*.

Points to Ponder:

The *Sefer HaKuzari* writes that it is not permitted to say anything bad about *Eretz Yisrael*. One may not criticize the water, food or air. We should appreciate *Eretz Yisrael* as the most beautiful country in the world.

Once, a terrible epidemic spread through Yerushalayim and Chevron. Many Jewish children died. The Jews of Yerushalayim went to *tzaddikim* to find out what they could do to stop the epidemic. The holy *tzaddikim* of Yerushalayim said that "the Fathers had the power to stop the suffering of the children." The leaders understood this to mean that they must go to *Me'aras HaMachpeilah* to beg the *Avos* to go before Hashem and request mercy for "their children."

There was just one problem. The Jews were not allowed into the *Me'aras HaMachpeilah*. The rav of Chevron, the revered R' Chaim Chizkiyahu Medini, spoke to Shimon Hausman, a wealthy Jew who was respected by everyone for his honesty and kindness. Together they came up with a plan. One of the many Arabs to whom Shimon had loaned money was a guard at *Me'aras HaMachpeilah*. The Arab had already been unable to repay the loan for many years. Shimon planned to threaten the Arab with imprisonment — unless he allowed him to enter *Me'aras HaMachpeilah*. If he allowed Shimon to enter, the debt would be canceled. The plan worked perfectly. The Arab was terrified at the thought of allowing Shimon to enter the *me'arah*, but the thought of not having to pay the debt proved too inviting. They agreed upon the night of Yom Kippur.

The night of Yom Kippur arrived. Shimon and his friend, R' Mordechai Eliezer Weber, dressed as Arabs. Trembling with fear and the excitement at being the first Jews to enter the cave in hundreds of years, the two Jews silently followed the Arabs into *Me'aras HaMachpeilah*. The first large hall they entered was built on top of Avraham's tomb. (As mentioned previously, we cannot be absolutely sure which

People stopping to pray at the site of the seventh step

Where is the seventh step?

Today there is no longer a seventh step. If you look carefully at the right corner of the outside of the building, you will notice black stains on the stones. The black stains are from the soot of the many candles that were lit on this spot. This is where the steps were which used to lead directly into the cave itself. It has been recently discovered that the seventh step is directly opposite the burial places of the *Avos* and *Imahos*.

Today there are no longer steps leading directly into the cave. To enter *Me'aras HaMachpeilah* one must climb another set of stone steps which lead to the main entrance of the large halls built on top of the graves. However, many people still have the custom to stop and pray at the spot where so many prayers were offered for hundreds of years.

Site of the seventh step outside the Me'aras HaMachpeilah. The stone wall was blackened by the many candles lit over the years

In Our Times

In 1929 there was a terrible massacre in Chevron. Sixty-seven Jews were killed and hundreds were injured by the Arabs. Many of the victims were yeshivah students from the Slobodka Yeshivah. After that, Jews no longer lived in Chevron until the Six-Day War in 1967. During the Six-Day War the Israeli army captured the city of Chevron, and Jews entered *Me'aras HaMachpeilah* openly, in broad daylight.

hall is built on top of which grave.) They sat and said *Tehillim* with great awe and concentration. From there they went on to the halls of Yitzchak and Yaakov. Each precious moment was spent in prayer. When they heard the footsteps of the next guard, they slipped out through a side exit. The Jews of Chevron somehow learned about the midnight visit to *Me'aras HaMachpeilah*. They also saw that from Yom Kippur on, the disease mysteriously stopped.

The *Avos* had stopped the suffering of the "children."

Interesting Facts

Right after the Six-Day War a young girl attached to a rope was lowered into a narrow opening in the hall of Yitzchak and Rivkah. When she crawled out she claimed to have seen four gravestones. She was unable to go further because the tunnel was blocked with stones and sand. Interestingly enough, it was discovered that the tunnel ended right under the seventh step.

Miron / מִירוֹן

Grave of R' Shimon bar Yochai

Lag BaOmer, the eighteenth day of Iyar, is a special day on the Jewish calendar. It is not a *yom tov;* however, it is a day of great joy. On Lag BaOmer, which is the thirty-third day of the counting of the Omer, the twenty-four thousand students of Rabbi Akiva stopped dying. Rabbi Akiva was one of our greatest sages. He started learning Torah when

Entrance to the burial place of R' Shimon bar Yochai

he was forty years old. His wife Rachel sent him to yeshivah, where he learned for twenty-four years. When Rabbi Akiva finally returned home, twenty-four thousand students came with him. They were tremendous Torah scholars who learned Torah day and night. But Hashem was not happy with them. Since they were such great people, they should have truly honored and loved each other. Sadly, they did not have enough respect for one another. During the days of *Sefirah*, from Pesach until Lag BaOmer, Hashem sent a terrible plague. Twenty-four thousand students died, one after another. On Lag BaOmer the plague ceased. This, of course, is reason for great happiness.

Another reason is that this was the day when Rabbi Shimon bar Yochai died. In fact the day of his death is called *yoma d'hilula,* a day of celebration. Why celebrate such a sad event?

Before his death R' Shimon instructed his students that instead of a day of mourning, it should be a day of joy and celebration. And so it is. Every Lag BaOmer for hundreds of years Jews have flocked to the burial place of

Interesting Facts

There is a verse in large black lettering above the gate leading to the grave of Rabbi Shimon. The verse from *Chumash Devarim* states כִּי לֹא תִשָּׁכַח מִפִּי זַרְעוֹ, which means that the Torah will never be forgotten from the mouths of the Jewish people. Rabbi Shimon himself mentioned this verse, when he assured the other sages that the Torah will never be forgotten from the Jewish nation.

Inside the gravesite of Rabbi Shimon bar Yochai in Miron.

R' Shimon and his son on Lag BaOmer to attend the festivities at the grave. They are buried on a hilltop in Miron, a small town in the north of *Eretz Yisrael*. Miron is famous because of them. We sing songs about Rabbi Shimon and his son Elazar. It is a day of true joy and praying in the merit of the holy sage, Rabbi Shimon Bar Yochai.

Who was Rabbi Shimon?

After the death of Rabbi Akiva's 24,000 students, he started teaching again, to five great students. Rabbi Shimon was one of them. He learned from Rabbi Akiva for thirteen years in Bnei Brak and honored him greatly. This was after the destruction of the second *Beis HaMikdash* when the Romans ruled over *Eretz Yisrael*. The Romans were cruel people who wanted to take the Jews away from the Torah. They made all kinds of unjust laws to keep Jews from learning Torah and doing *mitzvos*. Rabbi Shimon bar Yochai once spoke against the Romans to a few other great rabbis. Someone who overheard him told the Romans what R' Shimon said. That was a terrible sin. Not only was it *lashon hara,* it put Reb Shimon's life in danger. The Romans wanted to kill Rabbi Shimon, and he and his son Elazar were forced to go into hiding. They hid in a cave near Pekiin, in northern Israel, for thirteen years. Hashem miraculously kept them alive by placing a carob tree and a stream of water near the cave. R' Shimon and his son ate the fruit of the carob tree and drank the water of the nearby stream. For thirteen years they did nothing but study Torah. Every day, twice a day, *Eliyahu HaNavi* himself would come to Rabbi Shimon and teach him the secrets of the Torah. With his son Rabbi Elazar, Rabbi Shimon wrote the Zohar, which contains hidden secrets of the Torah.

STORY CORNER

View of Miron and the gravesite of Rabbi Shimon bar Yochai on Lag BaOmer. The tents are pitched by visitors who have come to take part in the festivities of Lag BaOmer.

One day the sages were sitting in the *Beis HaMidrash*, studying Torah. One of the sages asked a question that nobody was able to answer. Rabbi Yehudah bar Ilai got up and said, "What a shame that bar Yochai is not with us, since he ran away from the Romans, and nobody here even knows where he is! "A few days later Rabbi Yosi, the son of Rabbi Yehudah, saw a dove flying in the sky. He stood up and called "Dove, dove — you are compared to the Jewish people. You are a loyal bird — since the days of the *Mabul*, the Flood." (After the Flood was over, Noach sent the dove to see if the land had dried up. It returned to Noach with an olive branch in its mouth.) Now Rabbi Yosi said, "Dove — go and give an important message to R' Shimon bar Yochai, at his hiding place." Immediately the dove flew down and landed at Rabbi Yosi's feet. Rabbi Yosi wrote the question on a piece of parchment and placed it in the

dove's mouth. The dove flew off and went to the cave where Rabbi Shimon was hiding. She beat her wings so that Rabbi Shimon would notice her. Rabbi Shimon saw the dove, took the parchment, and read the question. He and his son began to cry. They were sad that they had been forced to leave the other sages. Hashem sent *Eliyahu HaNavi* to comfort them and answer the question. Rabbi Shimon wrote the answer on the parchment and placed it in the mouth of the dove, which returned immediately to Rabbi Yosi. Rabbi Yosi took the parchment, and showed it to the other sages. He told them what he had done.

Rabbi Yehudah cried and said, "Lucky is Bar Yochai because Hashem does miracles for him. He will one day sit at the head of the *tzaddikim* in *Gan Eden*."

Finally, after twelve years in the cave, Eliyahu told Rabbi Shimon that he was not in danger anymore. He and Rabbi Elazer came out of the cave and saw everyone working their land, buying, and selling. Rabbi Shimon could not understand why they were not studying Torah instead. What could be more important than Torah? He stared at one of the farmers — and the man died! Of course, nothing is as important as Torah, but people must also work the land and plant and harvest. Otherwise they would die. A voice was heard from heaven. "Rabbi Shimon, have you come out of the cave to destroy My world? Go back to the cave!"

Rabbi Shimon went back to the cave for another year. When he came out he saw an elderly Jew carrying two bunches of sweet-smelling *hadasim*. Rabbi Shimon asked him, "What are these for?" "They are in honor of the Shabbos," answered the old man. "One is for the commandment to remember Shabbos and the other one is for the commandment not to work on Shabbos."

Then Rabbi Shimon understood that even everyday work is important, because it allows the world to exist. He also realized that Jews love their

Interesting Facts

- The building on top of the graves was built and paid for by Rabbi Avraham Galanti, a rich student of the *Ari HaKadosh*. Over the years changes were made. Both Rabbi Shimon and his son Rabbi Elazar are buried in the caves below. In the courtyard in front of the building itself is the grave of R' Yitzchak, an outstanding disciple of Rabbi Shimon. He is often mentioned in the Zohar. It is said that R' Yitzchak died the same day as Rabbi Shimon.

- On the roof of the building are two round iron containers in which the two bonfires are lit on Lag BaOmer. One bonfire is in honor of Rabbi Shimon, the other is in honor of his son, Rabbi Elazar.

G-d and fill their days with good deeds whenever possible.

Lag BaOmer is known as the *yoma d'hilula*, the day of celebration of Rabbi Shimon Bar Yochai. On this day R' Shimon called all of his students to his home. A fire surrounded his bed and his face shone with holiness. He taught them many secrets of the Torah that day, which are written in the Zohar.

At this time there was tremendous happiness in the world because

Lag BaOmer, fathers dancing with their three year old sons in the courtyard of Rabbi Shimon bar Yochai's burial place.

Interesting Facts

- **M**any Jews have the custom to take their three-year-old sons to give them their first haircut at the grave of R' Shimon bar Yochai on Lag BaOmer. This is called a *chalakah,* (or *opsheren* in Yiddish) which means haircut. R' Chaim Vital would tell how his Rebbe — the *Ari HaKadosh,* who learned many secrets of the Torah — went with his young son and family to Miron for the *chalakah.* Many Jews from all over the world travel to *Eretz Yisrael* to celebrate this occasion, when for the first time their little boy will have *payos,* by the grave of the holy sage, Reb Shimon bar Yochai.

Lighting candles at the grave of Rabbi Shimon bar Yochai

Hashem was allowing Rabbi Shimon to give over such holy secrets. The sun did not set at its regular time so that he would have more time to finish teaching. Rabbi Shimon then told his students that his soul was about to leave this world, and that instead of a day of sadness and fasting the Jews should celebrate this day as a day of happiness. R' Shimon was then buried in Miron, and since then people flock to Miron on Lag BaOmer to celebrate this special day.

STORY CORNER

In the year 1900, a very bright and G-d-fearing boy lived in the holy city of Yerushalayim. The boy's name was Shmuel Razin. Shmuel loved to learn Torah, and even at a young age he would spend many hours bent over the *Gemara*. One day a terrible disaster struck. Shmuel suddenly started suffering from a serious eye disease. His sight grew worse from day to day. One evening, while Shmuel was learning *Masechta Chulin*, a vein in his eye burst, leaving him totally blind. The last thing he had seen before that was the words, "And upon whom shall we rely? Let us rely upon Rabbi Shimon."

Weeks passed. Doctors and rabbis were consulted. No one was able to help. After a few weeks, Shmuel was sent to Chevron for a change of climate. There he was taken to see two great *tzaddikim*. One of them, Rabbi Chaim Chizkiyahu Medini, author of the *Sdei Chemed*, turned to Shmuel and asked him what was the last topic he had learned before he lost his sight. Shmuel responded that he had been learning *Gemara Chulin*, and the last words he had been able to see were, "Upon whom shall we rely? Let us rely upon Rabbi Shimon."

The two *tzaddikim* told Shmuel that that was his solution — the holy sage Rabbi Shimon bar Yochai himself. They told Shmuel to travel immediately to Miron and pray at the grave of Rabbi Shimon. Shmuel's uncle took him, and after many days of travel by donkey, they finally arrived in Miron. They went straight to the grave of Rabbi Shimon and remained there for several days, praying and crying without leaving even once.

One day Shmuel suddenly began to shout, "Uncle, I can see you!"

From day to day his sight improved. On the thirteenth day

Lag BaOmer in Miron. The Boyaner Rebbe lighting the bonfire with a torch.

he could see perfectly. Uncle and nephew left the grave dancing and singing songs of praise to Hashem and the holy sage, Rabbi Shimon bar Yochai. They sang, "And we — upon whom shall we rely? Let us rely on Rabbi Shimon bar Yochai."

After *Maariv* tens of thousands of people throng as close as possible to Rabbi Shimon's grave. The lighting of the bonfires takes place on the roof. Only the important people, including many leaders, both Ashkenazic

Question Corner

On the eve of Lag BaOmer, a *Sefer Torah* is taken from the house of Rabbi Shmuel Chai Abu in Tzefas. It is brought to Miron, to the grave of Rabbi Shimon bar Yochai. Where does this custom come from?

It all started about one hundred-sixty years ago. In 1834 there was a terrible earthquake in Tzefas. Over two thousand people were killed and the majority of the homes were destroyed. The Tzefas community was completely broken and utterly helpless. One man decided to take action. He was Rabbi Shmuel Chai Abu. He sent messengers to Persia and Turkey to collect money to rebuild the community. With this money he rebuilt houses for people to live in. He also provided food and clothing for those who had lost everything in the terrible earthquake. To show their appreciation to Rabbi Shmuel, the residents of Tzefas decided to give him a *Sefer Torah*. Everybody donated something, and they hired a *sofer* to write the *Sefer Torah*. They presented it to Rabbi Shmuel with a beautiful cover adorned with silver.

Rabbi Shmuel was very happy with his precious gift, and he asked that the *Sefer Torah* always and Sephardic, are allowed onto the roof. Traditionally the honor of lighting the two main bonfires has gone to the dynasty of Ruzhiner rebbes. The present Boyaner Rebbe is from this family. After the lighting, the music begins to play. Many songs are sung throughout the night in honor of Rabbi Shimon. Inside the building groups of people take turns praying, while outside in the courtyard there is singing and dancing.

In the courtyard many fathers are dancing with their three-year-old boys. They have come to the grave of Reb Shimon on Lag BaOmer for their *chalakah.*

The singing, dancing, and praying continue throughout the day. Great rabbis, yeshivah students, businessmen, government officials and even taxi drivers are all part of the crowd dancing together in honor of Rabbi Shimon bar Yochai. Women watch the dancing from a separate section. This gathering is truly a wonderful sight to behold.

In the *Gemara,* Rabbi Shimon bar Yochai is called *Rabban shel nisim,* master of miracles. Many stories are told about miracles which have taken place at the tomb of Rabbi Shimon. There are stories of women who did not have children for many years, who came to his grave to pray. A number of them gave birth within a year after promising to make a contribution in honor of Rabbi Shimon. Many of these women named their first-born sons Shimon.

remain in his shul. In those days, people would travel to Miron from Tzefas to spend Shabbosos at the grave of Rabbi Shimon bar Yochai. They asked Rabbi Shmuel if they could borrow the *Sefer Torah* and take it to Miron just for Shabbos. Rabbi Abu could not refuse them, and so the *Sefer Torah* would travel back and forth from the shul of Rabbi Shmuel to Miron every week. As a remembrance of those days, the custom was started many years ago to take the *Sefer Torah* of Rabbi Shmuel every Lag BaOmer to the grave of Rabbi Shimon. The *Sefer Torah* arrives right before the lighting of the bonfires and signals the beginning of the festivities.

IN OUR TIMES

What happens on Lag BaOmer?
The preparations for Lag BaOmer begin several days before. People begin arriving in Miron from all over *Eretz Yisrael.* They pitch tents and settle down to wait for Lag BaOmer. Some people even come a few weeks before Lag BaOmer and spend the time praying and learning. On Lag BaOmer itself over ten thousand sandwiches are distributed by the *Hachnasas Orchim* society of Miron. The celebration itself actually begins a few miles away, in Tzefas, on the night of Lag BaOmer. A *Sefer Torah* is taken from the house of a famous Sephardic family named Abu and brought to Miron.

Safed / צְפַת*

The holy city of Tzefas is in the Galil — the northern part of *Eretz Yisrael.* The ancient city is built on a mountain. Our sages tell us that after a person dies his soul goes before the *Beis Din shel Maalah,* the Heavenly Court, and is asked several questions. Among these questions the person is asked צָפִיתָ לִישׁוּעָה, did you long for the *Geulah?* While all Jews wait for the *Geulah,* the people of Tzefas are especially famous for awaiting the arrival of *Mashiach,* who according to the Zohar will first appear in the Galil. This is one of the reasons Tzefas is called by this name: Tzefas comes from the same root as *Tzipiyah* — waiting and hoping.

The city of Tzefas has winding streets and alleys, many of them leading up to old and beautiful shuls. On the mountainside of Tzefas itself is a very old cemetery dating back to the *tannaim,* our sages who compiled the Mishnah. For hundreds of years great Torah scholars and kabbalists, *tzad-*

*Pronounced *Tzefas* or *Tzefat*

*Typical alleyway in the Old City of Tzefas.
Walking single file is often a must!*

Left: Interior of The Avuhav Shul in Tzefas

dikim who study the secrets of the Torah, have lived in Tzefas.

Among them was R' Yosef Karo, who wrote the *Shulchan Aruch,* which contains the *Halachos* that tell us how to live our daily lives. *Mahari bar Rav,* the teacher of Rabbi Yosef Karo, and the *Remak,* Rabbi Moshe Kordovero, also lived there. Many of these great people are buried in the cemetery on the mountainside of Tzefas.

The grave of the *Ari* is in the old

The aron hakodesh in the synagogue of R' Yosef Karo

STORY CORNER

Almost five hundred years ago the *Ari HaKadosh* and his holy students would go out to the field every Friday right before Shabbos. Dressed in white clothing, their holy faces shining, they would greet the Shabbos queen. The *Ari HaKadosh,* whose full name was R' Yitzchak Luria Ashkenazi, and his students studied Kabbalah, the secrets of the Torah, written in the holy Zohar. They settled in Tzefas because it was close to Miron, the burial place of Rabbi Shimon bar Yochai, the holy sage who wrote the Zohar.

The *Ari HaKadosh* was born in Yerushalayim in 1534 and was descended from *Rashi.* The story is told that before his *bris,* Eliyahu *HaNavi* instructed his father to wait for him before starting the *bris.* The day of the *bris,* all were gathered — the *mohel,* the *sandek,* family and friends. The Ari's father refused to begin. Everyone sat and waited for a long time until finally, the Ari's father's face lit up and he signaled the *mohel* to begin. Eliyahu *HaNavi* had arrived.

The *Ari* lost his father at the tender age of eight, and he and his mother moved to Egypt, where she raised him with the help of his uncle. He learned from the *Ridbaz,* R' David ben Zimra, and Rabbi Bezalel Ashkenazi, who taught him both the revealed and secret parts of the Torah.

cemetery in Tzefas. Close by is the *mikveh* where he would immerse himself. The waters of this *mikveh* are from a natural spring flowing through the rocks of the ancient hills of Tzefas. These waters are ice cold. It is said that the *Ari* promised that any person who immerses himself in his *mikveh* will not leave this world without doing *teshuvah*, repenting.

STORY CORNER

One Erev Shabbos when the *Ari* and his students went to the fields to greet the Shabbos queen, the *Ari* suddenly clapped his hands and, turning to his students asked, "Would you like to greet the Shabbos queen in Yerushalayim?" Some of the students were taken aback and said that they first wanted to go home to tell their wives. The *Ari* began to tremble and cried out, "The opportunity is lost! We could have been in Yerushalayim to greet the Shabbos queen."

Some say that if his generation would have been worthy, he would have had the power to bring the *Geulah*.

Right: The grave of the Arizal as it appears today after renovation. Beside it we see the grave of R' Shlomo Alkebetz, author of the famous song Lechah Dodi in the Friday night prayer. Below: The grave of the Arizal before renovation.

The mikveh of the Arizal

STORY CORNER

In the year 1834, a terrible earthquake struck the Galil. The city of Tzefas was nearly completely destroyed and thousands of people died, buried under buildings and caves. At the exact time of the earthquake, Rabbi Yaakov Ninyo, a great *tzaddik* and kabbalist, was praying from a *siddur* in one of the shuls. His *siddur* was not an ordinary one — it was handwritten by the Rashash, Sar Shalom Sharabi, himself. Many years before, the great kabbalist the Rashash, had given this *siddur* to one of his students as a protection and guide. It was a holy *siddur* with many writings of Kabbalah. Over the course of many years, the *siddur* had passed from hand to hand and it was now in the possession of Rabbi Yaakov Ninyo — who was standing and praying at the moment of disaster. He heard the terrible grinding sounds of the earthquake and bent over. Burying his head in his hands, he recited the *Shema*. When it was over he was standing under open sky holding his *siddur*. The entire building was in ruins, and the other fifty men praying with him had died instantly, buried under the rubble — but he was safe!

DID YOU KNOW?

That many of our Shabbos *Zemiros* come from *tzaddikim* who lived in Tzefas? *Lechah Dodi* was written by Rabbi Shlomo Alkabetz, and the Ari wrote *Azamer Bishevachim, Asader LeSeudasa* and *Bnei Heichala. Kah Ribon Olam* and *Yedid Nefesh* were also written there.

There are two shuls in Tzefas called the *Beis Knesses HaAri*. One is the Sephardic *Beit Knesset HaAri*. When the *Ari HaKadosh* moved to Tzefas, this shul was already built. He chose to pray there because of its location; it overlooked Miron, the burial place of Rabbi Shimon bar Yochai. Also, on one side of the shul was the cave of Eliyahu *HaNavi*. The *Ari* would enter this cave in order to study the secrets of the Torah and merit גְּלוּי אֵלִיָהוּ, when Eliyahu *HaNavi* would reveal himself to the holy Ari.

The Ashkenazic *Beis Knesses HaAri* is also known as חֲקַל תַּפּוּחִין קַדִּישִׁין, *the field of holy apples*. It is called by this name as the shul was built on the site of what used to be a large orchard. This orchard was called "the field of holy apples." It was here that the

Entrance to the Sephardic Beit Knesset HaAri

The aron hakodesh of the Chakal Tapuchin synagougue, the Arizal "Ashkenazi" shul.

Ari and his students would come every Friday before Shabbos to greet the Shabbos Queen. After the *Ari's* death, the Ashkenazic community in Tzefas decided to build a shul in the name of the *Ari* on this holy site.

Many years after the *Ari* died, he appeared in a dream to one of the *tzaddikim* in Tzefas. He said that people were using his room in the shul and sitting in his place. He asked that nobody enter that room. From that time on the room was closed off, and is no longer used.

Only some portions of the Sephardic and Ashkenazic shuls are the original buildings. This is because in 1834 there was a terrible earthquake in Tzefas. Close to two thousand people died and many shuls and buildings were destroyed — including parts of the *Ari* shuls.

There are also many other famous shuls in Tzefas. Among them is the *Alshich* shul. Rabbi Moshe Alshich was among those *tzaddikim* who had the word *HaKadosh,* the holy one, added to their names. The holy *Alshich* lived most of his life in Tzefas and was a talmid of Rabbi Yosef Karo. The *Alshich* would give weekly *parashah shiurim* which many people came to hear. Later

STORY CORNER

The *Alshich* very much wanted to join the *Ari's* group of students, who learned the secrets of Kabbalah from him. The *Ari* refused to accept him. The *Alshich* begged and begged, and finally the *Ari* agreed that he would be able to join for one *shiur.* The *Alshich* was very excited, but when the time came and the *Ari* started teaching, the *Alshich* promptly fell asleep! He woke up just when the *Ari* had finished teaching. The *Ari* told the *Alshich* that this was clearly a sign from Hashem that the *Alshich* should study Toras HaNigleh, the revealed parts of the Torah, and should not concentrate on Kabbalah.

Inside the Sephardic Beit Knesset HaAri

on these *shiurim* were published as *Toras Moshe,* a work that is most well known simply as *"The Alshich HaKadosh."* His shul was the only shul in Tzefas that was not destroyed in the famous earthquake of Tzefas. It remains standing until today.

Points to Ponder:

Did you know that although we mention the *Ari* most often in connection with Tzefas, he actually only lived there for two years? The *Ari* settled in Tzefas at the age of thirty-six. For two years he taught many secrets of Kabbalah to his holy students. The word *Ari* means lion, and *Gurei HaAri* means lion cubs. As Rabbi Yitzchak Luria Ashkenazi was called the *Ari*, his students were called *Gurei HaAri*, or lion cubs. At the young age of thirty-eight, the *Ari HaKadosh* returned his holy soul to Hashem.

Right: an artist who takes pride in his work. His special job is to paint and maintain the graves in the cemetery of Tzefas.

Below: the ancient cemetery in Tzefas

STORY CORNER

In 1572 a terrible epidemic swept through Tzefas. Many people died. The *Ari* instructed his students and their families to remain in a group of houses sharing one courtyard, without any contact with the rest of Tzefas. There the students would spend their days in peace and harmony, and learn Torah from the holy *Ari*. This peaceful arrangement went on for some time, and no one from the group became sick. One day two little boys began fighting. Instead of stopping the argument, the mothers of the boys entered the fray, each one angrily defending her son. A shouting match followed and even the husbands, students of the *Ari*, became embroiled. The peace of the courtyard was shattered. When the *Ari* was told about the fight he began to tremble. He had promised his students protection from the epidemic only as long as they learned together in peace and harmony. A short while later several students became ill. The *Ari* himself became sick and died.

Water in Eretz Yisrael

The many bodies of water with which Eretz Yisrael is blessed.

Panoramic views of the Kineret

Kineret/Sea of Galilee

This bright blue lake is right next to the city of Teveria, which was named for the Roman Emperor Tiberius. Teveria is one of the most beautiful cities in *Eretz Yisrael*. Many great *tzaddikim* lived and are buried there. The *Chida* writes that the twenty-four thousand students of Rabbi Akiva who died during *Sefirah* are buried in the mountains of Teveria.

A view overlooking Teveriah and the Kineret

During the forty years that the Jews spent in the Wilderness, there were no lakes, no rivers, and no water. Hashem made a great miracle, in honor of Moshe's sister Miriam. A well, which was situated in a big rock called Miriam's Well, went with the Jews in the desert. All of the water the Jews drank in those forty years came from that well. Today that well lies somewhere in Lake Kineret, although we don't know exactly where. The waters of the well of Miriam are supposed to be able to heal people from sickness.

Question Corner

Why is this lake called Kineret? Because of its shape. It is wide in the north and narrower at its southern end, just like a *kinor* or violin.

STORY CORNER

There was a Jew living in Teveria who had terrible boils all over his body. One *Motzaei Shabbos* his wife went to draw water from the Kineret. She filled her bucket with water and walked carefully home. As she was entering her home the bucket slipped off her shoulder and water splashed everywhere. Wherever a droplet fell on her husband's body, the boils went away. It is said that this water came from the well of Miriam.

Yam HaMelach
The Salt Sea/The Dead Sea

Yam HaMelach is mentioned in the Torah as part of the southern border of the tribe of Yehudah and *Eretz Yisrael*. It is also right near the cities of Sedom and Amorrah, which Hashem destroyed because they were so wicked.

At Yam HaMelach

DID YOU KNOW?

• The water of the *Yam HaMelach* is thirty-five percent salt! It is the saltiest spot on earth. Even the salty oceans are only about six percent salt. For this reason, when bathing in *Yam HaMelach,* one has to be careful not to get water into the eyes or on an open scratch, because the salt can burn terribly. *Yam HaMelach* is also the lowest body of water in the world. At its highest point it is about 3,000 feet below sea level. Many rare minerals are found in this sea. Many people with skin diseases, arthritis and other sicknesses travel to *Yam HaMelach*. They bathe in its waters and it makes them feel better. In fact, the *Gemara* mentions that people used to swim there for their health. It is one of the blessings that Hashem gave *Eretz Yisrael*. It is almost impossible to drown in the *Yam HaMelach!*

A glimpse of Yam HaMelach through a crack in the wall of the fortress at Masada.

Sunrise at Yam HaMelach, against the magnificent backdrop of desert mountains

STORY CORNER

When the Emperor Vespasian came to the *Yam HaMelach* he wanted to see if it was true that one could not drown there. He commanded his servant to tie the hands and feet of a few men who could not swim and throw them into the sea. Not one of the men drowned! That is because the salt keeps people from sinking into the water — but you must be very careful never to drink the salty water!

Maayan Elisha/Spring of Elisha

Opposite the hills of Jericho is the famous Spring of Elisha. The people who lived in this area once came to the *Navi* Elisha and complained about the water. They said that the waters from the spring were making people die. Elisha filled a small jar with salt and went to the source of the spring. There he threw the salt and said, "Hashem says that the water is healed.

A section of the Spring of Elisha in Yericho

Never again will it cause death or sickness." The waters immediately became healthy and once again people were able to drink it without worrying.

As Elisha was leaving the place, he noticed some young men standing in his way. These young men used to provide the people of the city with healthy water by bringing it from far away and selling it for a large profit. Now that Elisha had cured the water, they were out of business and very angry. Instead of asking him for help or discussing their problem nicely, they began to shout and curse, "Go up, bald head! Go up, bald head!" They were making fun of Elisha, who was bald. Elisha turned and looked at them carefully. He saw that they were totally wicked. Elisha cursed them in the name of Hashem and two wild bears came crashing out of the forest. The bears killed forty-two of these wicked youths.

DID YOU KNOW?

Neither bears, nor a forest
לֹא דֻבִּים וְלֹא יָעַר

According to some sages the miracle was that although there was a forest near Yericho, there were no bears in the forest. According to other opinions it was a double miracle — there was neither a forest nor any bears in the Yericho area. And yet when Elisha cursed the youths the bears appeared from nowhere!

Epilogue:
Land of Our Past,
Land of Our Future

Our sages tell us that whoever walks four *amos* (about eight feet) in the land of Israel will have a portion in the World to Come. For many Jews throughout the generations, taking those steps was the dream of a lifetime. Many Jews bend down and kiss the holy soil when they first arrive. Reading about *Eretz Yisrael* also awakens that desire within us.

Wherever in the world we live, our true home is *Eretz Yisrael*.

The mystery of Tzefas, the beauty of Teveryah, the majesty of *Midbar Yehudah*, the holiness of Miron — all are part of our land and our hearts. The Torah calls *Eretz Yisrael* the land of milk and honey, a place where the honey oozing from ripened dates will mix with the milk dripping from fat, healthy goats. *Eretz Yisrael* is also praised as the land of Seven Species with which it is particularly blessed: Wheat, barley, grapes, figs, pomegranates, olives and dates.

View overlooking the cemetery from the mountainside of Tzefas

Some of the Seven Species with which the Holy Land is blessed: Above: Olive trees Below: A grove of date-palm trees in Yericho. The palms of these trees are used as lulavim. Facing page: Pomegranate trees.

Despite its small size, *Eretz Yisrael* has a wide variety of landforms. Mountains and valleys, streams and rivers, deserts and rocky land are all found in this small country.

In the winter, pure white snow covers the peaks of Mount Chermon in the Golan Heights, in the north of the country. King Shlomo called Mount Chermon the lions' den and the mountains of leopards, because lions and leopards used to live there.

More of the Seven Species:

Left: A boy romping through a barley field.

Below: Bales of hay in a wheat field.

Left: The
snow-capped
peaks of Mount
Chermon.

Below:
Lush fields
at the foot of
Mount Carmel
in Chaifa.

Mount Carmel in Chaifa, on the other hand, is covered with foliage throughout the year. Many different types of animals live on this mountain. Mount Carmel is where Hashem brought down a fire to consume the sacrifice of the prophet Eliyahu in order to disprove the idol-worshippers, showing that Hashem was the true G-d.

There are also many rivers in *Eretz Yisrael*, such as Kishon, the largest river in the North. It was on these banks that the battle between the Jewish judge,

Above: Dusk at the Kishon port in Haifa

Below: A grotto at Rosh Hanikrah

Facing page: Waterfall at the Banias

Barak and Sisera, the Canaanite general, took place.

There are cliffs and caves, such as Rosh Hanikrah at the north, bordering Lebanon. There is a narrow tunnel carved into the cliff of Rosh Hanikrah which leads to windows in the rock, from which one can see the sea. This area was the home of the

chilazon, a type of snail which produced *techeiles. Techeiles* is a special blue dye, which was used to color one of the strings of the *tzitzis.*

Even in the barren, dry land of *Midbar Yehudah,* the Judean Desert, which stretches for many miles, there is variety. Here, Ein Gedi, with its rich plant-life and large supply of pure water, serves as an oasis in the barren desert. King David praises Ein Gedi in his book of *Tehillim,* when he describes how the springs flow between the hills, quenching the thirst of the animals. *How great are Your creations, Hashem, all were made with Your wisdom.* It was here that David secretly cut off the corner of King Shaul's robe while Shaul slept, in order to prove that he did not seek to harm him.

We are connected to *Eretz Yisrael* from our very beginnings as a nation.

Hashem told Avraham to walk through the length and breadth of *Eretz Yisrael,* so that it would be easier for his children, the Jewish nation, to conquer it.

Eretz Yisrael was the land of the prophets and land of our sages.

Through the land we are connected to our roots, our past. But most of all, we are connected to the holiest of cities — Yerushalayim. Our sages tell us that ten measures of beauty

Previous spread: Majestic mountains in the Negev. At the left in the foreground, you can see the ruins of a Roman camp that besieged the fortress of Masadah.

Below: A section of the Jordan river

Facing page, top: The port of Acco

Facing page, bottom: Ruins of the ancient shul at Bir Am

Above: ruins of the mountaintop Herodian fortress of Masadah after the destruction of the second Beis HaMikdash. Below: mosaic floor at Masadah. Mosaics were a beautiful and popular form of artwork during the time of the first and second Batei Mikdash.

Aerial view of Masadah, one of the last Jewish strongholds after the destruction of the second Beis HaMikdash. Approximately one thousand men, women, and children held out in this fortress in Midbar Yehudah until the Romans closed in on them.

1. At the gravesite of Rabbi Meir Baal Haness in Teveria.

2. An aqueduct at Ceasaria, dating back to the time of the Roman conquest of Eretz Yisrael. Their rule lasted from the destruction of the Second Beis HaMikdash until the Byzantine Era. The Romans were accomplished architects who constucted many magnificent buildings, bridges and aqueducts. Some are still standing today.

3. Shoppers, tourists and Yerushalmi children in the Geulah neighborhood.

4. A section of the underground tunnels at the Kosel area.

5. A street scene in Yerushalayim's Meah Shearim.

6. *A medieval castle in Yerushalayim, built by the Crusaders in the twelfth century, during their occupationof Eretz Yisrael.*

7. *A Bedouin shepherd leading his flock in Harei Yehudah.*

8. *Colorful and informative posters of all sorts grace the stone walls of Meah Shearim and Geulah in Yerushalayim.*

9. *Purchasing esrogim in the streets of Geulah is an experience.*

10. *Montefiore's windmill in the Yemin Moshe section of Yerushalayim. The windmill was never actually used, although Montefiore had originally wanted the Jews around Yerushalayim to support themselves by using the windmill.*

Above: the caves at Qumran, where the Dead Sea Scrolls were discovered. These scrolls, as well as other artifacts, were preserved in the caves due to the Dead Sea climate.

were given to the world. Yerushalayim received nine, and one tenth was left for the rest of the world. Yerushalayim is the city where one's prayers are directly opposite the holy throne of Hashem. That is where the *Beis HaMikdash*, the most holy place in the world, stood.

Yet Yerushalayim, and of all of *Eretz Yisrael*, are not just links to the past. While many of our forefathers, sages, and leaders are buried there, the holy land is very much our focus for the future.

We are a nation that never loses its faith in Hashem. Every day we pray for our ultimate return. There are yeshivos for *Kohanim* in *Eretz Yisrael* which devote all their time to the study of sacrifices, so that the *Kohanim* will be knowledgeable and prepared when *Mashiach* comes. And we anxiously await the day when Hashem will restore the glory of Yerushalayim and gather the exiled to their home. As Hashem promised Rachel *Imenu*, "One day your children will return."

Father in heaven — let Your children come home.